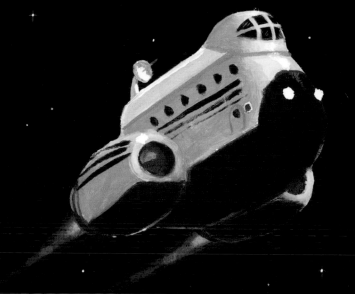

Field Trip
to the
Moon

by JOHN HARE

MARGARET FERGUSON BOOKS
HOLIDAY HOUSE · NEW YORK

To Henry, who inspires me
to be a better person.

To Evan, who reminds me that being
a better person should
include some dancing.

Margaret Ferguson Books
Copyright © 2019 by John Hare
All Rights Reserved
HOLIDAY HOUSE is registered in the U.S. Patent and Trademark Office.
Printed and bound in June 2019 at Toppan Leefung, DongGuan City, China.
The artwork was created with acrylic paint.
www.holidayhouse.com
First Edition
3 5 7 9 10 8 6 4 2

Library of Congress Cataloging-in-Publication Data
Names: Hare, John, (Children's book illustrator), author, illustrator.
Title: Field trip to the moon / John Hare.
Description: First edition. | New York : Holiday House, [2019] | "Margaret
Ferguson Books." | Summary: In this wordless picture book, a girl is
accidentally left behind on a class trip to the moon.
Identifiers: LCCN 2018024186 | ISBN 9780823442539 (hardcover)
Subjects: | CYAC: School field trips—Fiction. | Moon—Fiction. | Stories without words.
Classification: LCC PZ7.1.H3675 Fi 2019 | DDC [E]—dc23
LC record available at https://lccn.loc.gov/2018024186

ISBN: 978-0-8234-4253-9 (hardcover)

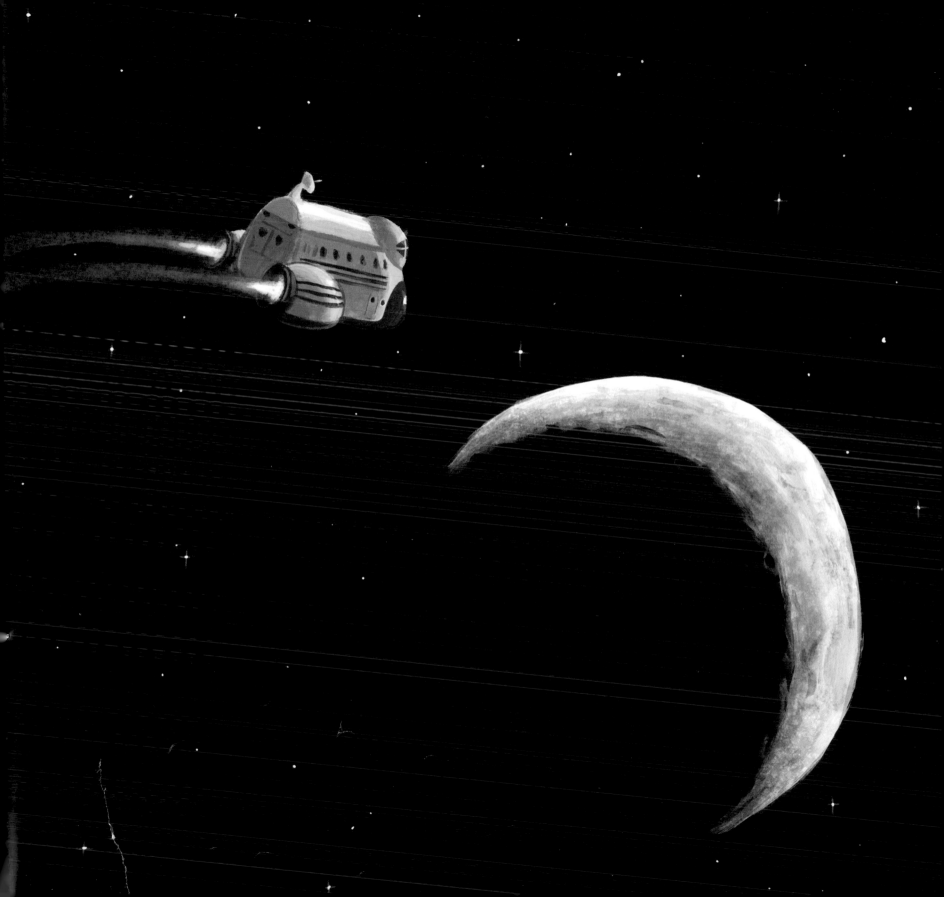

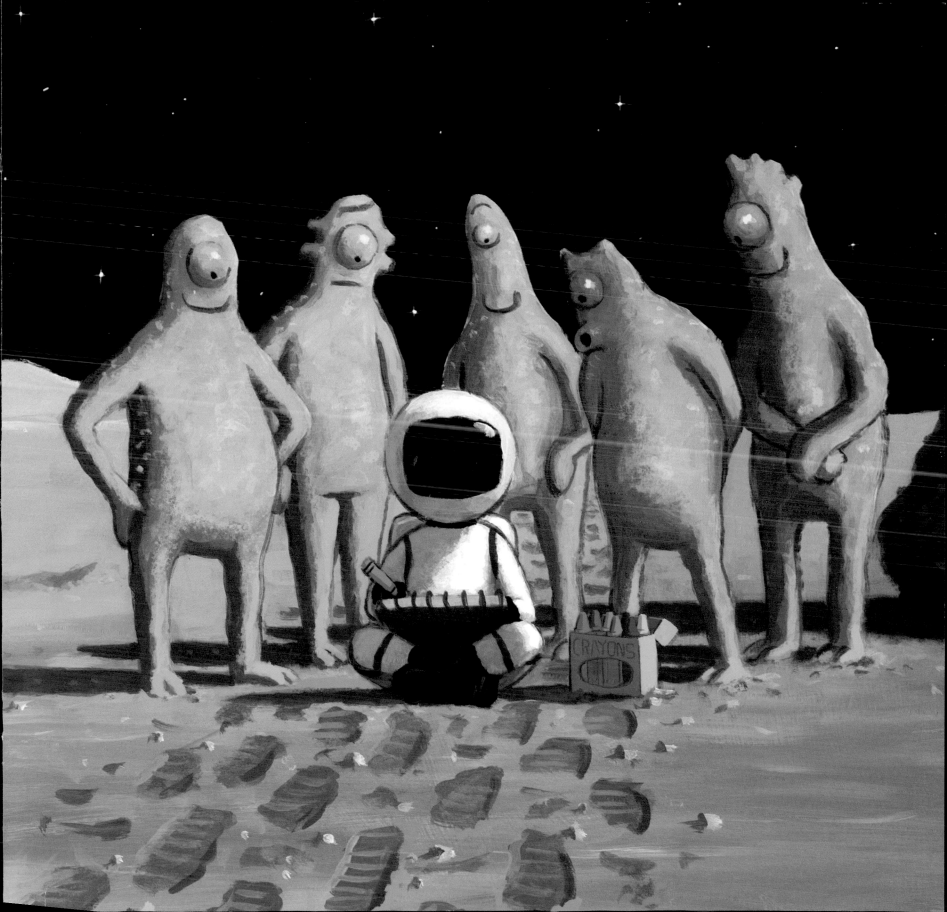

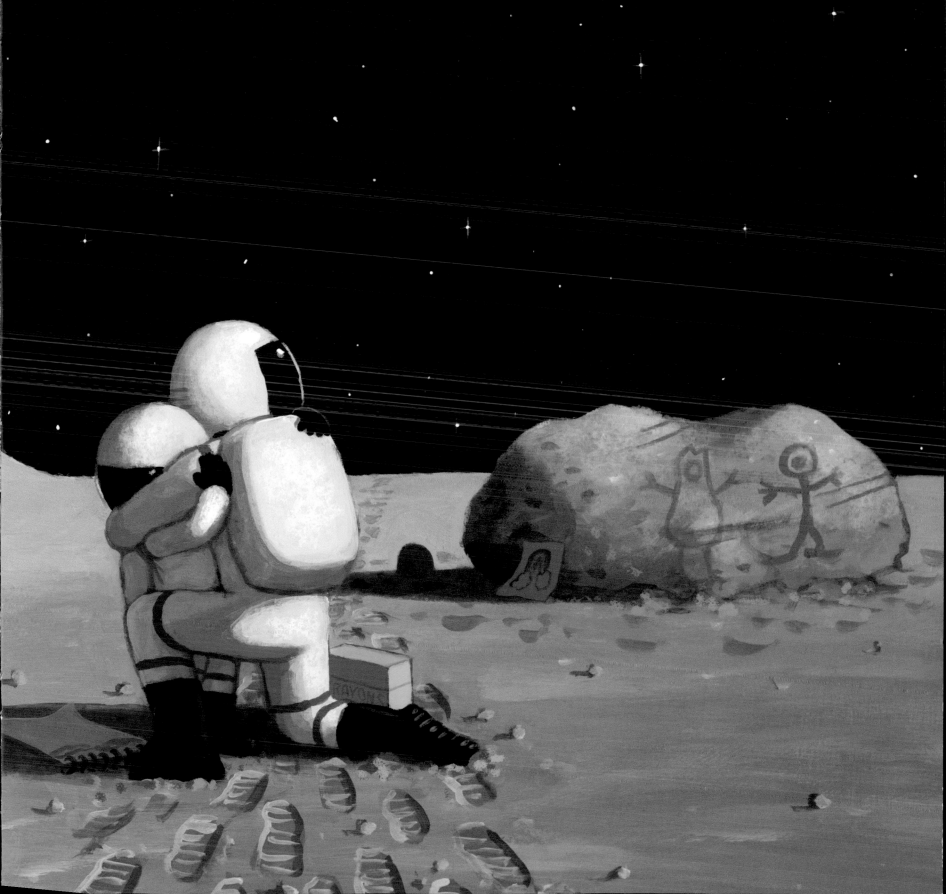

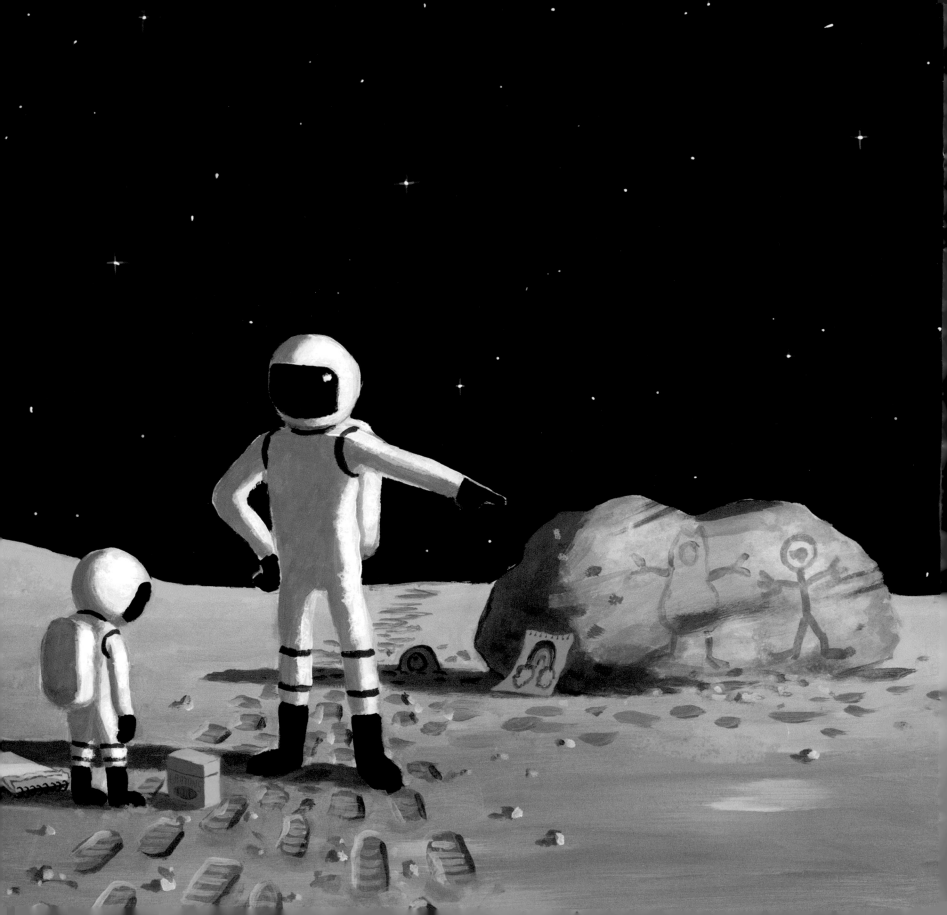